Mia, a six-year old girl, lived with her parents in a big house with an equally big lawn in front of it.

'ميا، الطفلة الصغيرة التى فى السادسة من عمرها كانت تسكن مع ابويها فى بيت كبير واسع امامه حديقة كبيرة واسعة .

Born with a loving nature, Mia loved to help her mother with the housework on every holiday.

بما ان طبيعتها ودية فكانت ترغب فى مساعدة امها فى اعمال بيتها كل يوم عطلة .

"ميا" المتوحدة
The Lonely Mia

English - Arabic

Carol Smith

Smith, Carol
The Lonely Mia
Dual language children's book

© Star Publishers Distributors
     ISBN: 81-7650-096-8

Published in India for
STAR BOOKS
55, Warren Street,
London WIT 5NW (UK)
Email: indbooks@spduk.fsnet.co.uk

by
Star Publishers Distributors
New Delhi 110002 (India)

Peacock Series
First Edition: 2004

Editor: Manju Gupta
Designing by: Dots 'N' Lines
Arabic Translation by : Anis-ur-Rahman
Printed at: Everest Press

One day Father left Mia with her grandmother and took Mother to the hospital.

فى يوم من الايام اخذها ابوها الى بيت جدتها و تركها هناك و ذهب بوالدتها الى المستشفى .

After one week Father brought Mia home from her grandmother's house. On returning home, Mia found Mother lying in bed with a small, cuddly brother for her. Mia decided to call him Pia.

و بعد مدة اسبوع جاء الاب بـ 'ميا' من بيت الجدة . وعندما وصلت 'ميا' الى البيت رأت ان امها كانت مضطجعة على الفراش و معها اخ لها صغير جميل جدا . قررت 'ميا' ان تدعوه "بيا" .

Mia simply adored her brother and loved to hover around him.
But her parents, fearing that she might hurt him or wake him up,
always shooed her out of the room.

احبت 'ميا' اخاها بشدة وكانت ترغب ان تكون بمقربة منه كل وقت .
ولكن الابوين،خوفا من ان تؤذيه ، او توقظه من نومه ، كانا يطردانها الى
خارج الغرفة .

One day, Mia took her big, brown doll to her mother and asked,
"Ma, can you please stitch a frock for my doll?"
"Not now, Mia," replied her mother. "I have to feed your little brother."

وذات يوم اخذت 'ميا' دميتها السمراء الكبيرة الى امها و سألتها : "يا امى هل تخيطين قميصا لدميتى
هذه ؟" فردت امها قائلة : "ليس الآن ، انى أرضع اخاك الصغير هذا الوقت ."

A bit disappointed, Mia went to look for her father. Father was busy in the lawn. She went to him and said, "Pa, let's play hide and seek." Father replied, "Not just now, Mia. I have to remove the weeds and mow the lawn. Why don't you go out and play?"

مایا با عصبانی پیش پدر آمد. پدرش درباغ مشغول کار بود او به پدر
گفت ''بابا بیا بازی کنیم''
9   پدر گفت ''الان وقت ندارم باغ راتمیز می کنم. شما چرا بیرون بازی نمی کنی؟''

Mia went back to her room and tried to keep herself busy by playing with her toys.

مایا به اطاق خود برگشت و با اسباب بازی خود بازی کرد و وقت را می گذرانید.

A few days later, Mia went to her mother to say, "Ma, let's go to the market. You had promised to buy me a new pair of shoes."

Mother replied, "Mia, how can I leave your little brother and go? He will miss me. Ask your father to read out a story to you."

بعد از چند روز مایا به مادر گفت، "مادر! بیا برویم بازار. شما برای خریدن کفش به من قول دادید."

مادر گفت : "مایا چطور می توانم برادر کوچک شما را بگذارم و بروم. ایشان بدون من نمی تواند بماند. به بابا بگو که برای شما قصه بگوید."

A trifle sad, Mia went in search of her father. She found her father resting on a sofa. She went to him and said, "Pa, I've brought this book. Please read out a story to me."

"How can I do it now, Mia? Last night I couldn't sleep a wink as your little brother kept on crying. You go and do your homework."

مایا کمی ناراحت شد و به دنبال بابا رفت دید که او در حال استراحت است ایشان پیش بابا رفت و گفت "بابا از این کتاب برایم یک داستان بگویید" "من چطور می توانم قصه بخوانم مایا! دیشب من اصلاً نخوابیده ام چون برادر شما خیلی گریه می کرد. شما برو درسهایت رابخوان." پدر جواب داد.

A thoroughly disappointed Mia went back to her room, thinking that her parents cared only for her brother Pia. Feeling sorry, she said to herself, 'No one loves me any more. Since the day Pia has come to the house, Ma and Pa have stopped caring for me.'

ناراحت مایا به اطاق خود رفت. ایشان فکر کرد که مادر و پدر او فقط فکر برادر هستند. با رنجیده از خود گفت حالا هیچ کس ما را دوست ندارد. از وقتی که

13   برادرم در خانه آمده، پدر و مادر در فکر من نیستند.

So one fine morning, she had her breakfast and soon
returned to her room.

يك روز صبح او در حال صبحانه خوردن بود و به زودى
به اطاق خود برگشت.

Packing a few things like a tooth-brush, a comb, a frock and a cake of soap in a small bag, she tip-toed out of her room and out of the house.

ایشان مسواک، شانه، صابون و پیراهن خود را جمع کرد و از اطاق خود بیرون آمد.

On reaching the door, she looked around the lawn and her eyes fell on the dog-house lying in a corner, a few steps away from her home. It belonged to her pet dog Bonzo. She hid herself inside the dog-house. 'No one will be able to find me here,' she thought.

بعد از رسیدن دم در ایشان به طرف باغ نگاه کرد. او دید که کمی دور تر بونذو سگی خانگی در کنار باغ دراز کشیده است. او فکر کرد اگر اینجا خود راقایم کند کسی نمی تواند او را اینجا ببیند.

At lunch-time Mother came to look for her and not finding her in her room, began to call out,"Mia! Mia!" But Mia was nowhere to be seen.

عندما كان وقت الغداء ، جاءت الام تبحث عنها ، و عندما لم تجدها فى غرفتها بدأت تنادى : 'ميا' ! 'ميا' ! ولكن 'ميا' لم تكن هناك لتجيب .

Mother went rushing to Father's room and told him,
"Mia is not in the house. Where could have my little girl gone?"

اسرعت الام الى غرفة الاب وقالت له : ''ميا' ليست موجودة فى البيت ،
اين يمكن ان ذهبت بُنيّتى ؟''

Father got up and both of them went
searching for her from one room to another,
calling out,"Mia! Mia!" But there was no reply.

قام الاب و ذهب كلاهما يبحثان من غرفة الى اخرى
يناديان 'ميا' ! 'ميا' ! ولكن لا جواب هناك .

Mother and Father then rushed out to the lawn, calling out to her by name. On hearing their voices, Mia held her doll to her heart and began to sob softly.

ثم خرج الاب و الام كلاهما الى الحديقة يناديانها باسمها . فلما سمعت 'ميا' اصواتهما بدأت تبكى وهى تضم لعبتها الى صدرها ، حتى انها بدأت تنشج بخفة .

On hearing a muffled sound, Mother said to Father, "Can you hear something?"
Father nodded his head. Both went in the direction of the dog-house. There they found
Mia sitting, with tears streaming down her eyes.

عند سماع صوت غامض قالت الام للاب : "هل تسمع شيئا ؟" حرك الاب رأسه ان نعم . فذهب
الاثنان الى اتجاه بيت الكلب و وجدا 'ميا' هناك جالسة و الدموع تجرى من عيونها .

Father picked her up in his arms and hugged her. Mother too rushed towards her, asking in a choked voice, "Why did you run away from us, Mia? You know very well we can't live without you."

اسرع الاب اليها و ضمتها الام اليها . وهى تسأل بصوت مختنق لماذا هربتِ منا يا 'ميا' ؟ انك تعرفين جيدا اننا لا نستطيع ان نعيش بدونك .

That evening, while changing Pia's clothes, Mother asked Mia to wave the rattle to keep her baby brother amused. At night, Mother put her to bed while Father read out the story Mia wanted to hear.

وفى نفس اليوم مساء ، عندما كانت الام تغيّر لباس 'ميا' ، قالت لها حرّكى الشخشيخة ليتمتع اخوك و يتسلى و فى الليل ، اخذتها الام الى الفراش ، بينما قرأ لها الاب القصة التى كانت 'ميا' تريد ان تسمعها .

Before leaving the room, Mother asked Mia,"Tomorrow morning, we'll go to the market to buy you a pair of shoes. What colour shoes do you want? Blue or red?"
"Red!" shouted Mia with joy.

قبل ان تخرج الام من الغرفة قالت لـ 'ميا' ''نذهب بكرة صباحا الى السوق لشراء الاحذية لك . اى لون تحبين ؟ ازرق او احمر ؟''
''احمر'' ، صوّتت 'ميا' بفرح .

With her cup of happiness full to the brim, Mia fell off to sleep, dreaming of a fairy in a red pair of shoes.

بقلب هادئ ، مملوء فرحا و سرورا ، غطت 'ميا' فى النوم تحلم بحورية جميلة لابسة حذاء احمر اللون جميلا .